Mr. Bumba's

NEW

HOME

By Pearl Augusta Harwood

Pictures by Joseph Folger

Published by Lerner Publications Company · Minneapolis, Minnesota

Copyright © 1964 by Lerner Publications Company

Manufactured in the United States of America.
Published simultaneously in Canada by
J. M. Dent & Sons Ltd., Don Mills, Ontario.

Standard Book Number: 8225-0101-5
Library of Congress Catalog Number: 64-19770

Third Printing 1966
Fourth Printing 1967
Fifth Printing 1969

Mr. A. C. Bumba was an artist.

He was a painter of pictures.

When the policeman went to his police
station, Mr. Bumba stayed at home and made
pictures.

When the storekeeper went to his store,
Mr. Bumba stayed at home and made pictures.

When the milkman went off in his milk truck, Mr. Bumba stayed at home and made pictures.

When the mailman went off with his mail bag, Mr. Bumba stayed at home and made pictures.

When other men went to the office to work, Mr. Bumba stayed at home and made pictures.

He made pictures on large white paper, with paint of many colors.

What did he make pictures of? Oh, a little of this, and a little of that, or anything he liked very much to look at.

One day he made a picture of Mrs. Jones peeling potatoes out in her backyard.

One day it was a picture of Mrs. Smith looking out of her window.

And once he painted the clothes on Mrs. Bobbett's clothesline. Mrs. Bobbett did not like that one so much.

What did Mr. Bumba do with his pictures?

He hung them up in an empty store
downtown for people to see. He put them all
along the walls of the empty store. So the store
wasn't empty any more. It was full of Mr.
Bumba's pictures.

One by one, people bought Mr. Bumba's
pictures. Then he kept on making more pictures.
He loved to do it. It was his work.

Mr. Bumba painted his pictures in a little room in Mrs. Jones' house. It was a very small room. He ate in it and slept in it too. When he cooked his breakfast he bumped into his bed. When he made his bed he knocked over his brushes. When he finished painting a picture he didn't know where to set it to dry. His room was <u>very</u> small.

One day Mr. A. C. Bumba got a letter. It was from his Aunt Mary.

The letter said,

Dear A.C.,

I am going to live with my friend in her house. So I am giving you my house.

I want you to come and live in it.

You will like it in this city. There are many people here who like pictures. So please come soon.

From your loving Aunt,

Mary

So Mr. Bumba said good-bye to Mrs. Jones.

"You will find someone else to live in my room and pay you rent," he said to Mrs. Jones.

He said good-bye to Mrs. Smith.

"Don't forget to watch everything outside your window," he said to Mrs. Smith.

He said good-bye to Mrs. Bobbett.

"No one will be here to make a picture of your clothesline," he said to Mrs. Bobbett.

They all said to Mr. Bumba, "Have a good time in the city. Make a lot of pictures, Mr. Bumba. Good-bye, Mr. Bumba, good-bye!"

So Mr. Bumba went to his Aunt Mary's house to live, and his Aunt Mary went to her friend's house to live.

Now Mr. Bumba had a whole house to himself.

"Now I can paint all day long," he said to himself. "There will be no one to bother me."

But he could not paint anything at all. He just sat there, looking at his white paper and his brightly colored paints.

And why couldn't he paint?

Because no ideas came to him. Because he saw nothing at all that he liked to look at.

He went out into his yard. He sat on the bench and looked at the grass. Then he heard some voices.

"What is the matter?" asked Jane.

Jane was looking over the high grey

fence at Mr. Bumba.

"What is the matter?" asked Bill.

Bill was looking over the high grey fence at Mr. Bumba.

Jane was on one side of Mr. Bumba's yard. Bill was on the other side. Mr. Bumba lived between Jane's house and Bill's house.

"Yes, what is the matter?" said Mr. Bumba. "Why don't I get any ideas for painting pictures?"

"Oh, please paint a picture!" said Bill.

"I can't," said Mr. Bumba, "I can't think of a thing to paint."

"Why?" said Jane and Bill, together.

Mr. Bumba put his head in his hands.

"Because all I can see is my grey house!" he said. "It is grey all over. It is grey inside, and it is grey outside. And the fence is all grey, all around this yard. I am feeling grey all over. I cannot paint a picture."

Mr. Bumba put his hands over his face.

"Don't cry, Mr. Bumba," said Jane.

"Please don't cry," said Bill. "We must think of something to help you paint pictures again."

"I wish you could!" said Mr. Bumba.

They sat beside Mr. Bumba on his bench. They put their heads in their hands. They thought very hard.

Then Jane began to jump up and down.

And Bill began to jump up and down.

They both had the same idea, at the same time.

"Why don't you cover up all the grey color with other colors?" said Jane.

"Paint the fence over," said Bill.

"And the outside of the house," said Jane.

"And the inside of the house," said Bill.

Mr. Bumba took his face out of his hands, and smiled a very large smile.

"Thank you, my dears, thank you!" he said. "And if you like, you may help me do it."

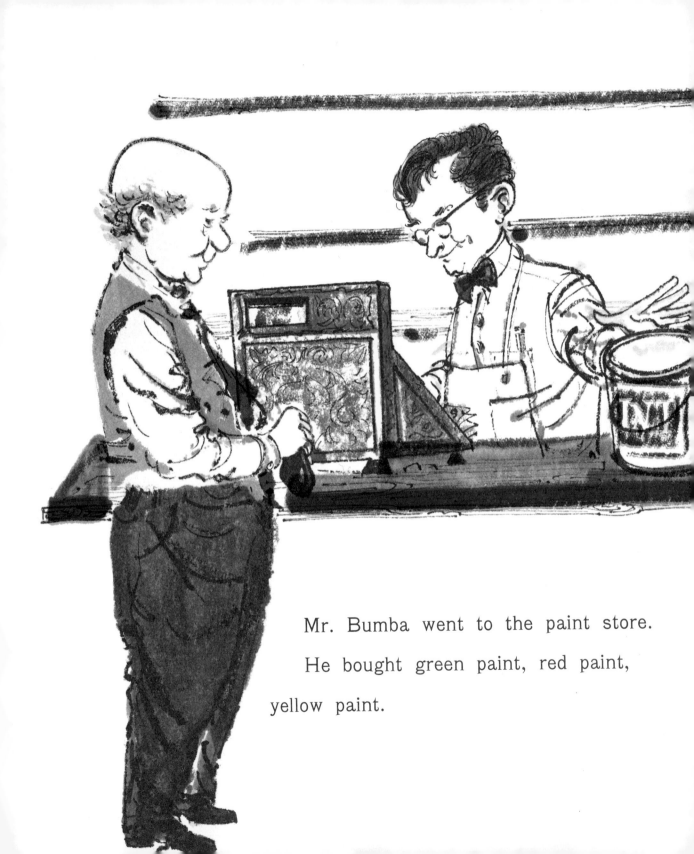

Mr. Bumba went to the paint store.

He bought green paint, red paint,

yellow paint.

He bought purple paint, brown paint, white paint.

He bought orange paint and blue paint, but NO GREY PAINT.

Every day Bill and Jane helped Mr. Bumba paint.

Soon the house was white all over, with green trimming.

Soon the kitchen was yellow.

Soon the living room was green.

Soon the bedroom was blue.

Soon the bathroom was pink and white.

"Now," said Mr. Bumba, "we'll do that big grey board fence."

"Let's make it orange," said Bill.

"No, let's make it purple," said Jane.

"Orange!"

"Purple!"

"Orange!"

"Purple!" Bill and Jane were shouting at each other.

"Hold on!" said Mr. Bumba. "I feel an idea coming. It's almost here."

They stopped shouting at each other. They looked at Mr. Bumba. He was smiling a very large smile.

"You two may rest now," he said. "I am going to paint pictures, all over that great big high grey fence!"

And he did. For days and days he worked
on the fence.

He painted mountains and rivers and oceans
and valleys.

He painted trees with squirrels, and meadows with cows.

He painted sky and clouds and sunshine and rain.

"There is just no stopping the ideas that keep popping into my head," said Mr. Bumba.

Soon people heard about the fence Mr. Bumba was painting.

They came from all over the city to see it.

They asked him to make them pictures like this part and pictures like that part. Then they bought the pictures from him. He had all the work that he could do.

And Jane forgot that she had wanted to paint the fence purple.

And Bill forgot that he had wanted to paint the fence orange.

They both wanted it to be just the way it was now. All full of pictures, all around Mr. Bumba's yard. It was just the kind of fence an artist should have.